Rainbow Bay

RAINBOW BAY

by Stephen Eaton Hume

illustrated by Pascal Milelli

RAINCOAST BOOKS

Vancouver

This is the house where I live
with my parents and my dog Scout.
It's on Rainbow Bay,
Silver Spring Island,
North America,
The Earth,
Milky Way Galaxy.

It's morning and the earth is new. Scout
yawns and scratches an ear. We look out the
window at Rainbow Bay. Water is flowing
out to the sea. The tide is getting low.

Things the sea had hidden
are coming into view.

Shells the color of sunrise appear on the shore.
Jellyfish blown across the ocean by trade winds,
and giant sea urchins from Japan, lie on the
rocks like jewels. Jutting out of the sand is a
wooden ship that sank in a gale a hundred years
ago. There's a bottle, too. I reckon a sailor
left it on the cabin table when he rushed
outside to say a prayer.

The water is only a trickle. The tide is
so low that if Scout and I wanted to we
could walk across to the other shore.
Periwinkles and moss-covered mussels
grip the sides of water-logged planks,
waiting for high tide. Long-legged
sandpipers dart across the flats,
chasing their own shadows.

We follow the tracks and find some
clams blowing bubbles in the sand.
Scout pushes his snout in the mud
like a snuffling pig and helps me
dig them out. A bucketful
for dinner!

I carry the bucket of clams up to the house. I pump cold water from the well into a porcelain basin and wash my face. Scout takes a drink. Then I stack firewood in an old wheelbarrow with rusty wheels. I race Scout to the wood hopper, but he wins. He always does.

I slice some bread and make a peanut butter sandwich and put it in my pocket. Scout and I walk down the road to the docks to watch the sailboats come in. Boats can reach the island, but cars and trucks are not allowed. Everyone on the island rides bicycles or horses. We ride in horse-drawn carts. We row. We canoe. No one's in a hurry here. The air is clean, and the sky is blue, not gray.

Scout and I make a path through the reeds, rustling the slender stems. I spy big webbed footprints. The way Scout growls and wags his tail you'd think a prehistoric creature had crawled from the water today, or maybe he's heard something I haven't . . .

We chase dragonflies through the
cattails. They buzz over the marsh, explode, flash
in the sun. They chase us back. Watch out! Attack!
We're ambushed by a flock of pterodactyls. Their
leathery wings beat the air. A griffin with eyes like
coals hovers over us and clacks its sharp beak. I
defeat the monsters in a sword fight. They
disappear, and only the hum of
their wings stays behind.

Breathless, we wait under a maple tree and watch
the clouds roll over as the wind sweeps across
Rainbow Bay. Scout digs a hole at the foot of the
maple and sprawls in the dirt. I lie down beside
him and share my sandwich. Above us the clouds
keep changing their shapes: now a schooner sailing
across the sky, now a sloop that trails a feathery
wake. The dirt is cool and comfortable. I can
smell the earth and the tree and the roots of a
wild sarsaparilla plant. The smell is like
a cellar of apples.

On to the strawberry patch! But we have to spot the berries first. They're hiding under the straw that keeps them warm at night. When we find them, the berries are sweet and fat, and ladybugs snooze on the leaves. I balance a strawberry on Scout's nose. He waits, snaps, and the juicy morsel disappears.

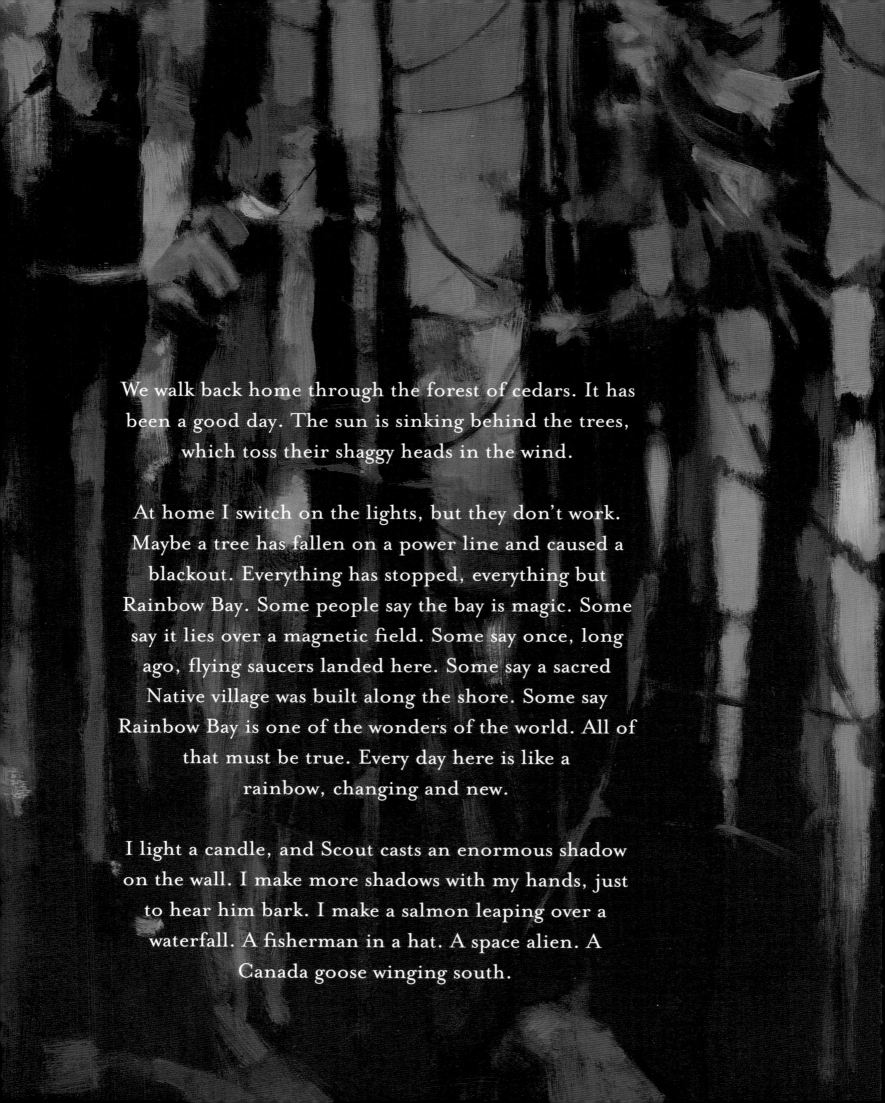

We walk back home through the forest of cedars. It has been a good day. The sun is sinking behind the trees, which toss their shaggy heads in the wind.

At home I switch on the lights, but they don't work. Maybe a tree has fallen on a power line and caused a blackout. Everything has stopped, everything but Rainbow Bay. Some people say the bay is magic. Some say it lies over a magnetic field. Some say once, long ago, flying saucers landed here. Some say a sacred Native village was built along the shore. Some say Rainbow Bay is one of the wonders of the world. All of that must be true. Every day here is like a rainbow, changing and new.

I light a candle, and Scout casts an enormous shadow on the wall. I make more shadows with my hands, just to hear him bark. I make a salmon leaping over a waterfall. A fisherman in a hat. A space alien. A Canada goose winging south.

The darkness has settled into the house.
We go outside and sit on a hill. The moon
is up. Soon it will be high tide.

Fireflies sparkle and leave luminous trails.
We see a star shower, and another, and
another. The heavens above Rainbow Bay
are spectacular tonight. The Pleiades
shine on, and Orion, and Orion's
hounds. Deer step out of the shadows and
gather on the hill. Scout stares at them
and shakes all over, but doesn't move
from his spot. Good dog, Scout.

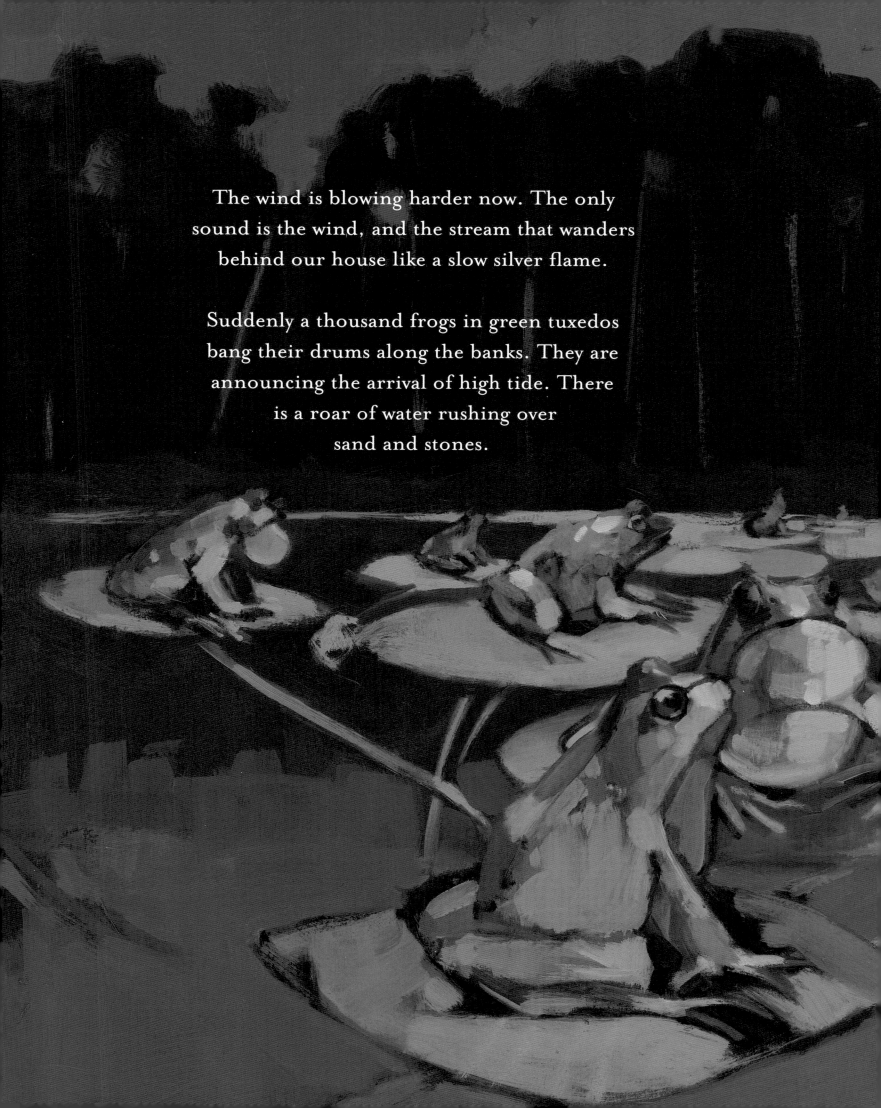

The wind is blowing harder now. The only
sound is the wind, and the stream that wanders
behind our house like a slow silver flame.

Suddenly a thousand frogs in green tuxedos
bang their drums along the banks. They are
announcing the arrival of high tide. There
is a roar of water rushing over
sand and stones.

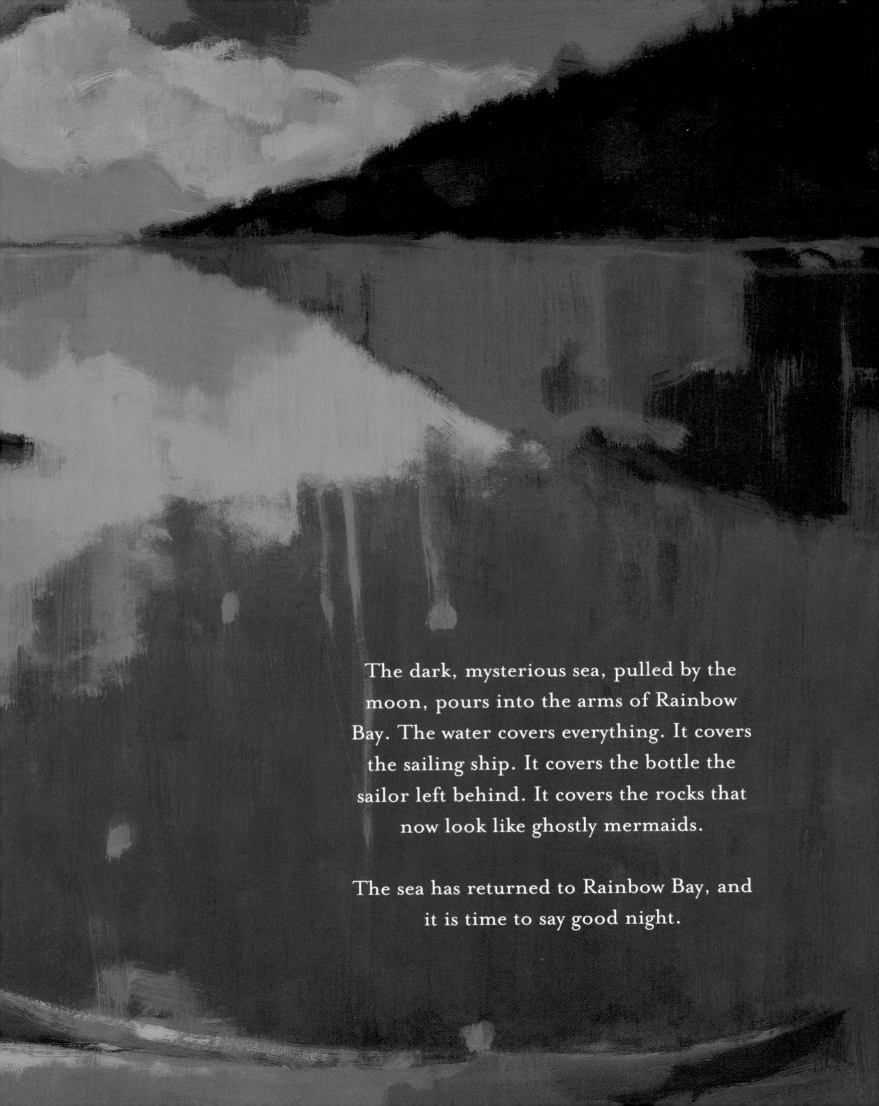

The dark, mysterious sea, pulled by the moon, pours into the arms of Rainbow Bay. The water covers everything. It covers the sailing ship. It covers the bottle the sailor left behind. It covers the rocks that now look like ghostly mermaids.

The sea has returned to Rainbow Bay, and it is time to say good night.

To my daughter Natalie, with love

– S.E.H.

To Olaf

– P.M.

First published in 1997 by
Raincoast Books
8680 Cambie Street
Vancouver, B.C.
V6P 6M9
(604) 323-7100

1 3 5 7 9 10 8 6 4 2

CANADIAN CATALOGUING IN PUBLICATION DATA

Hume, Stephen, 1947-
Rainbow Bay

ISBN 1-895714-75-3

I. Milelli, Pascal, 1965- II. Title.
PS8565.U556R34 1995   jC813'.54   C95-910327-9
PZ7.H85Ra 1995

Designed by Dean Allen
Edited by Michael Carroll

Printed in Hong Kong through Palace International

*Raincoast Books gratefully acknowledges the support of the Canada Council, the Department of
Canadian Heritage, and the British Columbia Arts Council.*